FEEL THE NOISE

M/M CONTEMPORARY ROCKSTAR ROMANCE

THE ROAD TO ROCKTOBERFEST 2022

ARIA GRACE

SURRENDERED PRESS

Surrendered Press

Feel The Noise

CONTENTS

1. Larson 1
2. Reed 9
3. Larson 19
4. Reed 27
5. Larson 33
6. Reed 41
7. Larson 49
8. Reed 55
9. Larson 63
10. Reed 71
11. Larson 77
12. Reed 89
13. Larson 99
14. Reed 107
15. Larson 115
16. Reed 121

Epilogue 127

Also by Aria Grace 133

1

LARSON

"Sir, please step to the side and wait right here."

I have to hold in a sigh as the TSA inspector motions for me to move out of the way of the people walking through the X-ray machine behind me. "Is there a problem?"

"Just wait right here, sir. I just need to confirm that you don't have any weapons on you."

As if. "No, my pockets are empty." I have on a pair of chinos and a polo shirt, just about the most boring outfit a person could wear. But after watching a few of those drug trafficking shows on the Travel Channel, I should have known better.

Drug mules are now mostly little old ladies or nerds like myself.

The man waves some kind of scanning wand in front of me, wielding it like an X-ray dustbuster of some kind. “If you can just spread your legs and hold your arms out at your sides.”

“Sure thing.” He’s just doing his job. He probably has to deal with shitty people all day long. I don’t want to be one of them, so I suck in a deep breath and count to ten, trying not to let my face look as annoyed as I feel.

After a somewhat inappropriate pat down and near-probing, I’m allowed to grab my carry-on and shoes off the conveyor belt and head toward my gate.

For the thousandth time in twenty-four hours, I curse my idiot brother for putting me in this situation. As usual, Pitch is fucking up his life and expects me to bail him out. And as usual, I’m the bigger idiot who is running to his rescue.

A part of me knows he’ll never stop relying on me if I always fix shit for him, but a bigger part of me likes being relied on. And this is something only I can help with.

Most twins aren't as identical as Pitch and I are. If we have the same clothes on and our hair looks similar, even our parents have trouble telling us apart. That was fun when we were twelve. But as grown-ass men, I didn't ever expect to get the call from my brother asking me to pretend to be him.

In public.

On stage in front of thousands of people.

But I guess I was giving him too much credit.

When my rockstar brother texted two days ago and asked me to be him at the biggest music festival of his career, I thought he was joking.

Like, legit out of his mind on some serious psychedelics. Sadly, he wasn't.

Pitch spent the past week in Vegas, partying like the next few days weren't the most important of his entire career, and now, as anyone could have predicted, he's fucked up his voice and has laryngitis. According to his doctor, he won't be able to speak above a whisper for at least a few weeks, and there's no way he can perform for at least a month, maybe longer.

This means he can't lead his band during Rocktoberfest, a huge music festival in the middle of the desert. A music festival that officially starts tomorrow. And because his band is already pissed at him for all the other times he's messed up significant opportunities for them, he can't tell them the truth.

Enter me.

The gullible brother who can be talked into anything because my own life is so damn boring that I need to live vicariously through my brother now and then.

Usually, that means watching his band play and pretending I have his kind of talent.

I never, in my wildest nightmares, imagined I'd end up on stage in front of a crowd of tens of thousands of people...singing. Pitch is the attention whore. I'm the guy in the background, not a frontman. And yet, I'm about to get on a plane and be the lead vocals for one of the hottest up-and-coming rock bands in the country.

A sheen of sweat erupts on my brow and temples as the oxygen seems to ease out of the busy airport terminal. Trying to maintain as much composure as possible, I slowly count to ten and suck in a deep breath as I walk toward my gate.

I will not have a panic attack in the middle of the airport.

Not only will it cause a mortifying amount of embarrassment for me, but it would also ruin this crazy little plan that Pitch and I have cooked up for me to sneak into the festival, pretend to be him, and sneak out without anyone realizing he wasn't actually there.

Right as I find an open seat near the waiting area for my gate, my phone buzzes in my pocket.

Of course, it's said idiot brother.

Lars, bro. You there yet?

No, I'm at the airport. I'll be boarding my plane in about an hour.

An hour? Why so early? If you wait >5 mins b4 boarding, you're wasting time.

I roll my eyes, amazed that we share 100% of our DNA. ***How many flights have you missed?***

Not enough to make it worth being an hour early.

Whatever. I'll text you when I get there. Your clothes better be waiting there for me. It's bad enough I'll have to buy ripped jeans and a long-sleeved shirt to hide my tattoo-free arms before I drive to the festival. I couldn't be mistaken for Pitch before leaving town, and I can't be mistaken for myself once I get to the festival.

Oh, what a web we weave...

Yeah. Show luggage arrived w/crew. They keep asking my ETA. What should I say?

That you fucked up again. ***My flight arrives just after two. From the airport, it's almost three hours maybe. So tell them by five thirty, just to be safe.***

530? Practice @ 6. They'll freak.

Well, you should've thought about that when you were partying all week. I can't make the plane or the rental car go any faster. I'll get there as soon as I can. And the less time I have to hang out with people who know Pitch, the better chance I have of not getting caught in my little charade.

Fine. Just hurry.

Yeah. I put my phone in my pocket because I didn't think he'd say anything else, but then it buzzed again.

And thanks, Lars. I know you don't wanna do this, but I appreciate you having my back. As always.

Don't thank me yet. There's still a high probability I'm gonna fuck this up for you. In my mind, that probability is about 99%, but he insisted we at least try. Whatever happens now is on him.

Nah, you're a better vocalist than me. Just wear the arm brace so you don't have to play, and you'll be fine.

Instinctively, I glance down at my carry-on, reminding myself that the soft arm brace I bought is safely tucked away in there. As lead guitarist, Pitch always puts on quite a show. There's no way I can play like him. Not only because I'm rusty, but I've never been as good on the guitar as my brother. The only way I can pull this weekend off is by faking an injury to make sure I don't have to get anywhere near a guitar.

2

REED

I'm not looking forward to this personal protection detail out in the desert.

Usually, when I get assigned a private security detail, they're in an air-conditioned casino or carrying bags for Beverly Hills debutantes. But this one isn't gonna be either cushy or chill. Literally.

I'm gonna be babysitting a wild rocker in the middle of a music festival for the next several days.

From what I understand, I'm basically being hired to make sure an out-of-control rockstar doesn't blow his band's shot at a big contract with a major production studio. Glass Bay Studio invited *Steel Sac* to the festival as an audition of sorts. And, as part of the option to sign, they insisted on retaining me to keep Pitch Monroe in line.

It's not my favorite way to spend a long weekend, but it pays well, and I could use some fresh air and sunshine. But now that I'm out here on the highway, I'm starting to get excited about the job. The road is full of muscle cars, lifted trucks, and tour buses heading to the festival site.

It's hard not to get caught up in the excitement of the festival.

Over the past twenty-four hours, I've done a good amount of research on this Pitch guy, and I'm gonna have my hands full with him. Just a few days ago, he was pictured with a harem of women hanging off him in a Vegas casino. The last Insta post I saw showed him loading out of a limo at a prominent strip club. Individually, those things are all fine. No harm done. But as someone who's known to partake in more than a few recreational drugs and enough alcohol to leave him blackout drunk on a regular basis, he's at risk of being influenced in a negative way this weekend.

But I've dealt with worse.

If all I have to do is literally keep his nose clean and make sure he doesn't do anything to screw up the band's performance, we should be okay. I'm not sure if he knows I'm coming, so that should be an interesting surprise for him.

When I finally approach the gate, I follow the signs for staff parking and drive my SUV along the outer fence until I am directed inside. The location for the *Steel Sac* crew set-up is clearly marked on the map on the crew app, so I slowly weave my way through row after row of tents, buses, and RVs until I find the rig I'm looking for.

Just as I'm getting out of my car, a white sedan pulls in behind me. I glance over my shoulder and then do a double take when I realize it's Pitch Monroe.

But he doesn't look anything like he does in his pictures. Not only is his hair shorter than it was a few days ago, but he looks so...healthy.

It always amazes me how some B-12 and oxygen shots will keep celebrities looking young because there are no signs of all the partying I know he's done recently. His bright blue eyes and sun-kissed skin almost glow.

When he opens the trunk to pull out his bag, he realizes I'm still staring at him. "Hi. How's it going?"

"Pitch, right? Hi, I'm Reed Marshall. Glass Bay Studio hired me to be your personal security for the festival."

"Wha—" His jaw drops, and he just stands there, staring at me like I'm speaking a different language.

"I guess they haven't told you." I take a step toward him so we're not shouting across the parking lot. "But they do this kind of thing all the time."

He clears his throat and shakes his head, still looking confused. "Um, no. This is the first I'm hearing about having a bodyguard."

"It's no big deal, really." Granted, no one else in his band has one, but I'm hoping he'll just go with the flow and he won't cause a scene. "I'm just here to make sure your adoring fans don't get too crazy." *And that you don't get too crazy with your adoring fans.*

He chuckles lightly as he slams the trunk closed. "I don't think that's gonna be necessary."

"Probably not." Definitely will be, unless he's too partied out from the past week. "So, I get a paid vacation, and you get someone to bring you water when you need it. Win/win."

He smirks but then seems to catch himself and he schools his expression. "Whatever."

Okay, that seems slightly more in line with my expectations of Pitch Monroe. "Need help with your bags?"

"No, thanks. I'm traveling light." He pulls his phone charger out of the front console and then locks up the car. "Where to?"

"Isn't that your bus over there?" I point to the rig to the right of an open shade tent.

He shrugs. "I guess. They all look alike."

As a car guy, I don't think any of them look even remotely alike, but I could see how a non-car guy wouldn't notice the details. "Yeah, I think that's it."

Pitch just stands there for a second before finally taking the lead and walking to the bus. When he reaches the door, he hesitates. After a glance in my direction, he knocks once and then pulls open the fiberglass door and storms inside. "Hey, bitches. Daddy Pitch is home."

Rolling my eyes, I brace myself for the days to come. Then I step inside the bus and close the narrow door behind me.

"The Pitch-ster is here." The guys all mumble some sort of greeting to Pitch, and he high-fives or half-hugs them as he makes his way through the common space to where the bunks are.

There's only one open bed, so he throws his bag onto it and turns back to the group. "What time is practice?"

The drummer, Slade Ryan, glances at me then turns back to Pitch. "So, I guess he's the babysitter we were warned about?"

"You were warned? Must be nice," Pitch mutters to himself, but I hear him.

Slade laughs. "If you were here yesterday, you would have gotten the memo. But it looks like his influence is already working. You've never asked about practice times before. Usually, we're dragging you out on stage, ten minutes late."

Pitch glances at me and then softly chuckles after relaxing his shoulders. "Yeah, I guess."

Slade turns back to me and gives me a once-over. "I'm Slade. Welcome to *Steel Sac*."

I wave somewhat awkwardly. "Hey, guys. I'm Reed. I'm mostly here to keep the fans in line. I'll try to stay in the background and out of your way unless you need me."

The second guitarist stands up and offers me his hand. "Hey, Reed. I'm Alex, but these guys usually call me Whip. Good to meet you."

"Hi, Alex...or, uh, Whip. Good to meet you too."

Rocco also introduces himself to me. The keyboardist is almost as hot as Pitch, but not quite. None of these guys are gay, so it'll be easy for me to keep things professional. But even I can admit there's something sexy about a guy in a band.

I read all about them from the band bios provided by Glass Bay, and they seem like cool guys in person. So far, it seems like a good gig.

Rocco opens up the fridge and pulls out a beer. "Reed, you want one?"

I shake my head once. "No, thanks. I'm on the clock."

He glances at Pitch then back at me. "Is Pitch allowed to have one?"

All the guys laugh, and I can see Pitch's cheeks pink up. Again, that doesn't seem like something that would embarrass a guy like Pitch, but maybe he's more sensitive than I'm giving him credit for.

Instead of answering, I look at my watch. "Didn't I see a text about practice starting in twenty minutes. Do you usually drink before you perform?"

They all laugh again, much louder this time, but Slade seems to be the voice of reason. "Yeah, you're right. We need to take this seriously, guys. We can celebrate after practice."

Grateful when they change the subject, I hop onto the driver seat and send a text to Erin, the assistant back at the office. ***I'm in the bus with Pitch. They have practice soon and then we'll see how the night goes. Where's my tent?***

Erin texts back with a map and photos of the fanciest glamping tent I've ever seen. There's a full-size bed, a refrigerator, and a TV set up inside. ***You're in 303. Everything you need should be set up, but***

let me know if you need anything else. Have fun.

I'm not sure fun is the right word to describe the next few days. But so far, it's at least uneventful. ***Yeah, it's going to be a blast.***

Erin texts back with a laughing emoji. ***I know you're being sarcastic, but it'll be great. Try to enjoy yourself. I know it's been a while, but I'm sure you'll remember how.***

Ouch. Not that she's wrong. I haven't been to a concert in years, so being paid to attend dozens of them isn't such a bad gig. I glance over at Pitch and am surprised to see him scrolling through his phone in the little sleeping compartment.

Maybe he won't be much trouble after all.

3

LARSON

A fucking bodyguard.

I keep stealing glances at the hot muscleman who was apparently hired to keep my brother in line. I should've known his reputation would ruin this little charade for me. Fortunately, these guys are all pretty self-centered, and having a stranger in charge of keeping "Pitch" in line means they don't have to pay too much attention to me.

Which is good because every word I say sounds forced and awkward.

Pitch and I are very different people. Since we were kids, I was the studious rule-follower, and he was the rebellious class clown. He'll do anything for a story, while I usually sit quietly in the background, ready to call for an ambulance.

Unfortunately, this time I have to be in the spotlight.

And I don't think any of the guys have noticed the brace on my arm yet, which means I have to break it to them. Just before we leave for the rehearsal, I clear my throat to get everyone's attention. "Hey, guys. I forgot to mention that I busted my arm up yesterday. I can't play tonight or probably at all."

"What the fuck, Pitch?" Slade is in my face, carefully probing my fingers to see if they're okay. "How long are you in this thing?"

"Doctor said a couple weeks. It's a hairline fracture, so I should fully recover, but...this show is out for me."

I turn to Whip, the other guitarist. "Which means this is your big moment, dude. You get to bring the whole show home."

He nods without saying anything, but after a few seconds, he seems to realize the opportunity that's being presented to him. "Yeah, okay. I got this. It won't be the same without you, man, but we'll be good."

Rocco smacks my shoulder and gives me a little shake. "Your vocals are good, right? No problem there?"

"Yeah, don't worry. I've been babying my throat all week."

Reed, the silent bodyguard in the corner, suddenly makes himself known with a snort and then tries to cover it up with a cough. "Excuse me. Got a tickle in my throat..."

By the way he's looking at me, I can't help but wonder if he knows my secret.

But he doesn't say anything, so neither do I.

Slade grabs his favorite sticks and a bottle of water from the fridge.

"Anyway, we should get going. Practice is starting soon."

Just then, one of the crew members bangs on the door and screams for us to get our asses to the sound stage.

Rocco claps his hands together and looks at each of us. "All right, guys. This is it. We're going to nail every note and make this the best set we've ever played. And then we're going to do it again tomorrow for real."

"Fuck yeah!" Whip jumps up and gives Rocco a noogie. "Let's do this shit."

I follow them out of the bus and to the soundstage. They've all been on site for at least 24 hours, so I have an excuse to let them lead the way.

Reed brings up the rear, stepping up to my side. "You excited?"

I turn to him, ignoring the way my cock is almost as attentive to his presence as my brain. "Yeah, definitely. It's a big deal for them...us. It's a big deal for us."

Reed cocks his head, looking at me with a probing gaze that I can almost feel underneath my skin. "Yeah, seems like it."

I speed up my pace to catch up with the other guys. Walking just behind them, I'm officially part of their group without having to engage in their random conversation.

Reed gets the hint and stays back, giving me space as we emerge from behind the stage onto one of the mid-sized platforms. As I grab an in-ear monitor, I hold my head high and try to look confident as I approach the mic stand.

I'm soooo not a performer. Not in public, anyway.

When Pitch and I were kids, back when he was just Patrick and I was just Larson, we used to play around in the garage with the equipment our dad set up for his percussion band. But no one but Pitch has heard me sing since I was twelve years old.

My stomach rolls, and I'm not sure if I'm gonna pass out or puke or both. But when the crew starts talking in my ear, I focus on what I'm there to do and get into position. *I can do this. I will do this.* I know all of *Steel Sac*'s music, and I can match Pitch's sound pretty closely, so when I hear my cue, I close my eyes and belt out the lyrics my brother and I wrote together just over a year ago.

The practice goes well, and when the guys all head to one of the party tents to eat and have a beer, I peel off and head back to the bus. I'm not used to the dust and my eyes are itchy. I need to find an antihistamine so I'm not trying to sing through phlegm during the big show.

I've almost forgotten about Reed until he steps into the rig behind me. "So, what's on the agenda for tonight?"

"Oh, hey." I pull down the t-shirt I was about to take off. I can't risk anyone seeing my bare skin or they'll know I'm not Pitch. He has *Steel Sac* tattooed across his chest and everyone knows it. Probably even the hot bodyguard. "I'm gonna just crash. If the studio felt the need to hire you, that probably means I need to keep a lower profile." Smiling, I realize how crazy that sounds, so I try to make it sound a bit more believable. "And my arm is hurting, so I need to just chill for a while. You can head out, if you want."

He grins like I'm trying to pull something. "Nah, I'm okay. Do you want to grab dinner? There's a taco truck that smells amazing."

"Is that what that is?" My stomach rumbles, and I realize I haven't eaten since breakfast. "Yeah, I could eat. Let me just change first." I feel stupid taking a clean shirt into the tiny bathroom to change, but it's either that or asking Reed to wait outside. And with the way he's looking at me, I'm pretty certain he knows something's up with me.

Though, I can't imagine he would ever guess that I'm not Pitch. No one ever goes there, even though the fact that we're twins is public knowledge. I'm just way too boring to ever be mistaken for my brother, which makes this even more exhausting.

When I come back out, Reed gives me a quick once-over then smiles. "Okay, then. Let's grab some grub."

4

REED

The garlic steak tacos we get are the best I've ever had. After my fourth one, I realize I need to slow down or I'm gonna be comatose in an hour.

All I can say about Pitch is that he's an enigma.

Without the band and the cameras in his face, he's a completely different person. He's calm and polite and nothing like his persona. Not only did he pay for my dinner, but he was more interested in chatting than I would've expected.

Honestly, I thought he would try to ditch me as soon as we got into the crowd, but he stayed right on my heels as I wove my way through the lines of people waiting to order. And when we finally found an open table that was on the outskirts of the area, he seemed visibly relieved. As soon as we were sitting down, he exhaled deeply and his shoulders relaxed, as if he was uncomfortable with all the people surrounding him.

After eating and small talk, I just can't keep my mouth shut about his duality any longer. "You know, you're not exactly what I expected."

Pitch grins and takes a sip of the beer he's been nursing for the past half-hour. "Is that so?"

I shrug and take a drink of my own beer. "Well, I watch the news. I know you haven't been babying your throat all week, so the fact that you were able to perform as well as you did is impressive."

His eyes light up and that light flush in his cheeks appears again. "Thanks. I guess I am a different person when I'm on stage."

I'm about to ask about his wrist when a horde of women appear behind him. They're all screaming his name and trying to get their hands on him. Mostly, they're reaching for his back and arms, but one particularly bold woman leans right up against his side and whispers something in his ear.

I can't hear what she said, but the horrified look on Pitch's face says it all. For whatever reason, he's not into it. Which is surprising because even I think the woman is hot.

Regardless, I'm here to keep him out of trouble and that's what I'm gonna do. I stand up and shoo the ladies back. "Okay, okay. That's enough. We appreciate your support, but Pitch needs some downtime right now."

They whine and don't move an inch until several other festival security staff start walking toward us. That's when the women finally disperse in different directions, blending in with the dark background.

Pitch's eyes are closed, and he's taking slow and shallow breaths.

I step up to him, worried he might pass out. "Are you okay? Need me to grab a medic?"

He shakes his head and holds up a hand when I reach for him. "No, I'm fine. I just forgot how overwhelming that can be."

"Yeah, I didn't even see them coming. They just...appeared."

He chuckles and takes one deep breath before seeming fully composed again. "Yeah, they do that. I know most guys love it, but I don't appreciate strangers touching me when I'm trying to eat."

"Noted. I'll do a better job of keeping an eye on things." I almost wink before I catch myself, remembering he's not gay and I'm on the clock.

Pitch cocks his head and looks at me. "I didn't mean it like that. You're doing a great job. I just...wasn't expecting that."

None of what he's saying makes a lot of sense considering this is his persona. Pitch Monroe travels with an entourage of women everywhere he goes. Whatever's going on with him, it's not his norm. Maybe he's just tired from the week he's had. No one would blame him if he were. "Do you want to head back to the bus and watch a movie or something?"

Now his grin is wide and seems totally genuine. "Yeah, that actually sounds perfect."

The rest of the band probably won't be back for hours, so Pitch and I get comfortable on the little sofa and turn on the satellite TV. It takes a minute to figure out the remote, but then he finds the program guide and flips through it. "Let me know if anything looks good."

I'm more interested in watching him than any movie, but that won't do either of us good. Instead, I try to find a movie that will keep my attention where it should be...not on Pitch.

We settle into an action film that we both have seen before, but it's a safe choice and easy to get distracted by. But Pitch surprises me yet again when, twenty minutes into the movie, he's curled up in a ball, fast asleep.

I can't help but imagine how things might've been different if we were on a date. Not only would he be curled up against me, but I would have an excuse to carry him to bed. But since this isn't a date, I spend the rest of the movie watching him sleep, mesmerized by the gentle sound of his breathing and the way his perfect features soften when he's fully relaxed.

His sleeves are pulled up slightly but not enough for me to catch a glimpse of the tattoos that I know are hidden beneath. Usually, I'm not into guys with tattoos, but I would kill to see his ink, even if I used it only as an excuse to get a glimpse of his bare skin.

When the movie ends, I gently nudge Pitch on the shoulder, waking him up so he can get to bed. He stretches his arms up high and wide then shuffles into the bunk as I watch him put himself to bed.

This band must have an impressive PR team because the man I just watched crawl into a bunk bed is definitely not the party animal I've seen tweaked out and debauched all over the tabloid sites.

5

LARSON

The guys wander into the bus sometime after 4 AM and make just enough noise to wake me up. I'm generally a heavy sleeper, but I've got to take a leak, so I get up quickly and then go right back to sleep. After a few more hours of rest, I finally drag myself out of bed, ready for breakfast.

There's a note taped to the inside of my bunk that makes me smile.

Hope you slept well.

Call me when you wake up.

Reed

His number is scrawled at the bottom, so I shoot him a quick text. ***I'm up and going to grab breakfast. No need to join me if you're still asleep.***

The response is immediate, as if he's been staring at his phone, just waiting for me to text. ***I'm up and hungry. Be there in two.***

OK. I quickly brush my teeth and change my shirt, foregoing a shower even though I'm gross from not showering last night. But I don't wanna make Reed wait for me.

I chuckle at how different his experience would've been if my brother were actually here. Pitch doesn't consider other people's time. Ever.

If I really want people to think I'm him, I should be more narcissistic. But I just don't have it in me. At least, not when I'm with people who don't know Pitch personally.

I step out of the bus, and Reed is just walking up with his hands in his pockets. Damn, he looks good. His tight t-shirt looks painted over his muscular arms and chest, and I want to run my fingers across the skin, learning every inch of his body. But Pitch doesn't swing that way. "Good morning."

His smile is bright, and it's almost like he's happy to see me...not just doing his job. When he looks at me like that, it feels like he's flirting. But my brother is a straight-up playboy, so Reed would be really stupid to try to flirt with him. Then again, I'm not my brother.

But I've never been a good gauge of guys, so who the hell knows. "Hungry?"

"Starved. And I've seen a train of breakfast burritos passing me by. Even from a few feet away, they smell and look amazing."

"Enough said." I step up beside him and gesture toward the food trucks. "Lead the way."

The lines aren't long, so we grab some burritos and coffee then find a table off to the side. There are a lot fewer people out in the morning than there were last night, and I'm happy to have this quiet time before a performance.

"Are you excited for today?" Reed takes a bite of his burrito and then looks at me, waiting for my response.

I finish chewing a bite as I nod. "Yeah, I am." Then I shrug and give him a sly grin. "And nervous as fuck."

He laughs out loud. “I think that’s the first time you’ve dropped an F-bomb when we were alone.”

Oh shit. Maybe I’m not being as “Pitch-like” as I thought. “I guess since I don’t know you that well, my mother’s insistence on us being polite and professional has kicked in.”

“Us?” He puts down the coffee cup he’s about to drink from and leans closer. “You mean you and your brother?”

Fuck. I really don’t want to talk about myself in third person. It’s hard enough talking about myself as if I’m Pitch. This is all starting to get confusing. “Yeah. But anyway, have you heard much about the other bands? I planned to check some out but just haven’t felt up for it.”

Reed just shrugs and looks around at the few people wandering in. “Not much. I think things are going well, in general. Only a handful of people had to be kicked out yesterday, so that’s good.”

My eyes go wide and I almost choke on a piece of egg. “Really? Why? I mean, why were people kicked out, not why was that good. But also, why is that good? I mean, isn't it better if no one gets kicked out?" My verbal diarrhea is in full swing before I hear myself and finally shut up.

The half-grin on Reed's face makes me insanely curious about what he's thinking, but of course, I can't ask.

He looks at me and waits, probably to give me time to babble on even more. But finally, he responds to all my questions. "From what I read in my security memo, there were a few fights and one guy was carrying a gun. He didn't brandish it and he does have an open-carry license, but he was drunk, so he was taken in. Nothing serious that I'm aware of, which is a good thing."

"Oh, got it." I successfully changed the subject, but now I'm even more nervous about the performance. "Are there a lot of guns here?"

He grins. "Well, it's legal in Nevada, so...yeah, probably. But don't worry. Most people seem to be just having a good time. If you're worried about your own safety, you don't need to be. That's my job."

Which brings up another point. "I've been meaning to ask, what specifically is your job? I mean, are you here to keep the girls away? Or 'party animal Pitch Monroe' away from the ladies? Or what?"

Reed sucks in a deep breath and looks me right in the eyes. "Honestly, I have no idea. You seem to be one of the most chill and respectful rockers I've ever met. I don't know why I was hired, but I'm glad I was."

Before I catch myself, I reach forward and rest my hand on his. "Me too."

Fuck, fuck, fuck!

How do I recover from that? Since I'm mostly done, I quickly jump to my feet and grab my trash. "I should get back and shower. Our set is early today, so I want to get ready. I'll text you when I'm ready to leave the bus."

Without waiting for Reed to respond, I head back the way we came at a fast clip. I'd love to run the entire way there, but I don't want to look like a lunatic. And Pitch doesn't run. He works out with a trainer to keep his physique in check, but he hates cardio of any kind.

I can feel Reed's eyes on me as he follows behind, but he gives me space, not getting close enough to crowd me. And as I climb up into the bus, I can't resist a backward glance at Reed, my sexy security guard who now thinks my straight brother is into him.

Damn Pitch and his fucking laryngitis.

6

REED

Uh, what was that...?

I basically chase Pitch back to the bus, with the feel of his touch still burning on my hand. That wasn't a *bro* touch. That was gentle...sexy. Okay, maybe I'm reading a little too much into a simple hand gesture, but I am definitely getting some kind of vibe from him.

Between the lustful stares—which I can now admit I've caught from him a few times—and his total lack of interest in the women who've thrown themselves at him, he's finally starting to make sense to me.

Pitch is a closeted gay man. Or maybe bisexual, considering he can't be that good of an actor when he's with gangs of women. But that touch wasn't just an innocent touch.

He wanted to touch me...to comfort me.

So why did he run?

As I glance up at the window, hoping to see Pitch looking out at me, I come to a decision.

I'm gonna make a move.

Nothing overt or obnoxious. I just need to come up with a way to drop a hint and let him know that I'm interested if he is. I've never considered hooking up with a client, especially while I'm in the middle of a job, but his show will be over tonight, and I'm being paid to be here for the next two days.

If he stays and wants to hang out, I don't see any harm in that.

Then again, once the show is over and he doesn't have to behave, maybe he'll sow his seed in his usual way. Wine, women, and song is how the saying goes, right?

Hoping for Pitch to want to hang out with me when he's no longer contractually obligated to is ridiculous, even in my head. So I focus on the security alerts being sent to all staff as I lean against the side of the bus. Today, there have been more fights and random people trying to hop the fences without paying for a ticket, so I'm grateful Pitch is lying low in the bus and not causing trouble out in the mosh pits.

About two hours before they're due on stage, Pitch sends me a text. ***I'm about to jump in the shower. I'll be heading to the stage in about forty-five minutes. You can meet me at the bus then.***

I don't want to leave, but I've got to piss and I could use another bottle of water, so I turn toward my tent. ***I'll get cleaned up and be back before you leave. Thanks for the heads-up.***

The dots to indicate a reply is being typed pops up immediately, but no message comes. After two full minutes of waiting, I get a simple response from Pitch. ***Anytime.***

Apparently, the desert is making me paranoid because instead of taking that one-word for the simple answer it is, I'm analyzing it for a deeper meaning. *Did he actually write more and delete it? Did he struggle to come up with an appropriate response? Was he just not paying attention and it took him that long to finish typing the word and hit send?*

I have no idea what's going through his mind, and I need to stop pretending I can guess what he's thinking. If he's interested, he'll tell me. And since I'm interested, I'm going to tell him. Not directly tell him, but I'll figure out how to drop a hint or two.

Either he'll pick them up or not.

My quick shower in the mobile bathroom is one of the most unsatisfying I've ever taken, but I'm clean where it counts, so I call it a win and quickly head back to the bus. Even though I was only gone for thirty minutes, the band is already filing out of it when I get back.

But Pitch isn't with them.

"Hey, guys." I nod at Slade, the closest thing I've seen to a leader of the group. "Where's Pitch?"

He points over his shoulder to the inside of the bus. "He's right behind us. You can go in."

When I go inside, I see Pitch sitting on the couch, leaning forward with his head between his knees.

"Hey, are you okay?" Immediately, I'm at his side with my hand on the back of his neck. "Can I get you some water?"

He nods and then shakes his head. "No, just sit here for a minute."

The rest of the band didn't seem worried about him, so I'm wondering if whatever is happening to Pitch right now began after they walked out. "Pitch, you're scaring me. What's going on?"

"I'm not..." He sighs heavily and shakes his head. "I just need a minute. I fucking hate being on stage, in front of people."

My jaw drops. "You're the frontman for a successful rock band. What do you mean, you hate it?"

He shrugs and his mouth opens a few times like he's about to say something, but then he changes his mind. Finally, he sits up straight and leans back on the couch. "Usually I'm fine. But I guess I'm just not feeling like myself right now. I'll be fine, I just needed a minute by myself to get my shit together."

Okay, that's fair. I'd be pretty freaked out too if I were about to give the most important performance of my career. Instinctively, I rub circles on his back. "What can I do?"

He turns to me and gives me a half-grin. "Just being here helps. Thank you."

I swallow hard and nod. "Well, then, I'm glad I'm here."

"Me too," he whispers, barely audible.

We sit quietly for a few minutes before he finally claps his hands together and stands up. "Okay, let's get this shit over with. I can do anything for an hour." He looks at his watch, and his eyes go wide. "Fuck. Slade is probably shitting bricks right now. We better go."

Pitch grabs a few things, and then I follow him out to the stage they're performing on. As we walk, he's standing closer to me than usual, close enough that his arm brushes against mine with almost every step.

Two women walk toward us and begin to giggle when they recognize him. As quietly as possible, I lean toward him. "Looks like you have a few fans approaching."

He groans and focuses on the ground right in front of him as we walk. “Oh god. They’re definitely not my type.”

Okay, this is my chance. Taking a risk that could cost me my career, I put my hand on his shoulder and give him a gentle squeeze. “I don’t know about that. If I were straight, they seem like they’d be my type.”

His eyes immediately lock with mine. At first, the shock on his face makes me think I’ve gone too far. But there’s no mistaking the lust in his gaze. “Maybe, but between you and me, my type is more like...you.”

My instinct, and by instinct I mean my dick, is telling me I should pull him into my arms and kiss him, but there’s no way in hell that would fly. Not here, not now. Instead, I wink and nod. “Ditto.”

Without another word, we head to the backstage area where the rest of the band is getting dressed and made up for their set.

I’m impressed by the production quality the studio is investing in for this show. These guys weren’t considered one of the top newcomers at the event, but you would think they were the headliner based on the team of stylists buzzing around.

Pitch gets shoved into a chair, and I'm quickly dismissed as they go to work on him. I want to pull up Google and search for anything I can find about Pitch Monroe being into guys, but I'm standing too close to all the radio equipment, and the shitty Wi-Fi out won't connect to the internet.

Frustrated, I slip my phone into my pocket and lean against a bench as I watch Pitch get transformed from sweet-and-sexy man who I can't stop thinking about to hot-as-fuck rockstar that I can't stop thinking about.

Much to my satisfaction, Pitch seems to be tracking my movements just as much as I track him.

Every time someone strikes up a conversation with me, I can feel his gaze burning a hole into my skin, and when I seek out his attention, it's always on me. Fuck yeah!

This job has definitely taken an unexpected turn for the better.

7

LARSON

I hit every note and didn't forget any lyrics.

That pretty much sums up what I can remember of the past forty-five minutes of my life.

As soon as we got on stage, everything became a blur, and I was just moving on auto pilot. I sang when I was supposed to sing, I said what I was supposed to say, and when the lights went out and the guys crowded around me, I knew it was finally over.

And based on the cheering and hugs I got from every person I passed on my way backstage, I think it all went well. But if I never have to sing in front of a stranger for the rest of my life, I'll die a happy man.

As soon as we're backstage, I see Reed from the corner of my eye. His eyes are beaming with pride, and the smile on his face is directly solely at me. Damn, I like how this feels.

Against my better judgment, I walk right into his arms and give him a hug.

Reed doesn't hesitate for a second, pulling me tight against his chest and breathing against my neck. "You were amazing. That was probably your best show ever."

Gathering my senses, I pull back and step away, leaving just enough space between us that it doesn't seem inappropriate. "You've watched us play before?"

"Not in person, obviously, but I watched a lot of videos when I was assigned this job. None of the shows I saw come close to how you looked just now."

Well, shit. I hope I haven't screwed up anything for my brother. I look at the rest of the guys, but they're drowning in trim and not at all interested in what the hell I'm doing right now. I shake out my hands, needing to release some pent-up adrenaline that's still flowing through me.

I turn back to Reed, wondering what happens next.

As if he can read my mind, he nods toward the back exit. "Are you done here? We can take a walk around and see who else is playing, if you want."

I nod and bounce a little on my feet. "Yeah, that sounds good. I'm still totally amped up."

"Let's go." His hand closes around my bicep and he gives me a gentle tug, pulling me through the crowd until we're free of the circus. Before we get too far, Reed looks back one last time and pauses. "Are you sure you don't need to stay for interviews or pictures or anything?"

I shrug. "Maybe. But I'm a wild card, right?"

He laughs and puts his arm across my back, pulling me into him for just a moment. "That you are, Pitch Monroe. That you are."

I want so badly to tell him I'm not Pitch.

It's on the tip of my tongue to come clean, but I can't. Not yet. I just need to get through the rest of the weekend, and then no one will ever need to know the truth. My brother can call the band on Monday with news about having laryngitis and no one will question a thing. I just have to keep my mouth shut a little bit longer. "Do you want a drink?"

Reed looks at me and then at his watch. "Technically, I was hired to keep you out of trouble until your show. Now that that's over, I think it's safe to have a beer."

"Good, cause I'm gonna have a few." I wink and turn us both toward the nearest concession stand.

Read raises an eyebrow. "Finally letting loose, eh?"

"I'm just glad it's over with. The past twenty-four hours have probably been the most stressful of my life. I think I've earned a couple drinks."

Reed and I each get a beer and a hotdog before heading toward the main stage to see who's playing. I've heard of most of the bands in the current line-up but don't follow any of them closely. Hard rock has always been Pitch's jam.

I mostly listen to pop and the occasional country station. My brother cringes every time he gets in my car.

We sit in on a couple shows, and when it starts to get dark, I realize that I might have had a few too many drinks. "Maybe we should get something more substantial to eat." I spin on my heel to head back toward the food trucks and stumble a bit.

But Reed is there, catching me and pulling me up against his chest. "Whoa there. Maybe no spinning for you for now, okay?"

I roll my head back and look at him. My mouth is just inches from his, and I'm so tempted to lean forward and kiss him. But I'm not that drunk. In fact, I barely have a buzz. Nothing a taco or some fries won't soak right up. "What about falling?" Shit, did that just come out of my mouth. Maybe I'm a little more buzzed than I thought.

Reed chuckles and shakes his head. "No, no falling either."

I lightly pinch his side and rest my head on his shoulder for just a second. "No, silly. I mean, falling for you."

His whole body goes still, and my brain catches up with my mouth a few seconds too late. *Fuck. What am I doing?*

Immediately sobering up, I pull out of his arms. "Just kidding, man. But I am getting hungry. Let's grab some grub."

The shocked expression on Reed's face quickly turns to confusion as he tries to keep up with my mixed signals. "Um, okay. Yeah, let's go."

We spend the next several minutes in silence, walking straight to a pizza truck that we both agreed earlier looked good and only speaking to place our orders. Once we have our food in hand, Reed looks around and then seems to come to a decision. "Hey, do you want to go back to my tent? It's quiet there and we can eat in peace."

Nodding, I shoot him a grateful smile. "Yeah, let's do that."

8

REED

I had zero intentions when I invited Pitch back to my tent.

Really, I thought we'd eat our pizza, maybe have a few more beers, and watch a movie. That's it. Nothing more seemed even remotely possible after the way he backed away from me earlier.

Besides, I thought he was a little drunk, so I wasn't gonna make a move.

But he's not drunk, and he's definitely hinting to make a move.

"Is it chilly tonight or is it just me?" Pitch crosses his arms over his chest and leans back against the head-board, shivering a bit.

I should offer him a jacket and leave it at that, but my little head is doing all the thinking right now, and my brain is just along for the ride. "Do you want to get under the blankets?"

His eyes scan me from head to toe and then back up to my mouth as he licks his lips and nods. "Yeah, that would be great."

We both slip off our shoes and climb under the down comforter and get cozy.

Pitch immediately snuggles up against my side, wrapping both of his arms around my bicep and clinging to me. "You're so warm. Your muscles must produce a lot of heat."

I don't know if that's a thing, but I'm not about to argue with him. "You know what they say about sharing body heat. If you're really cold, we can try that."

"Like, taking off our clothes?" Pitch looks so different from his persona. He's a totally different person when it's just us. Not only in physical appearance, but he's completely vulnerable while he waits for me to respond, like he thinks I might reject him.

"Yeah, if you want. But only if you're comfortable with that."

He doesn't say a word as his hands disappear under the covers and he shimmies out of his jeans. He leaves his long-sleeved shirt on, but it is a chilly night, so I don't question it. Although, I'm still curious to get a close-up and personal view of his notorious ink.

Following his lead, I slip off my jeans too. I consider leaving my shirt on, but I'm already heating up, so it follows my pants to the floor beside the bed.

Pitch's gaze skates over my chest, and he reaches for my bare skin, grazing it with his fingertips and sending shots of electric current straight to my cock.

As if he's being pulled to me like a magnet to steel, his chest crashes with mine and his mouth is on me, kissing me with everything he's got.

My shock and surprise lasts for about a second before I'm lowering him onto the mattress and hovering over his body. "Are you sure about this, Pitch?"

His eyes close for a moment, and then he looks at me with as much need and desperation as I feel for him. "Just kiss me, Reed. Please."

That's all I need to hear.

Lowering my body so my chest is resting on his without putting too much weight on him, I brush my lips over his, letting my tongue drag over the seam. Pitch's lips part in anticipation, and I groan as I slip my tongue inside, fully tasting him for the first time.

He moans and lifts his ass so his hard cock is pressed against my thigh.

"Fuck, babe. You're killing me. I'm trying to be a gentleman and you're not making it easy."

"I don't want a gentleman, Reed. I want you to fuck me."

My own dick is already thick and ready, desperate to blow inside his tight little ass. Our kisses become more frantic, lips and teeth trying to get even closer to each other. I nip his plump lower lip and then lick along his jaw. "I might have a condom in my bag, but I'm not sure if I packed lube."

I definitely wasn't expecting to get laid at this event. The only reason I have condoms with me is because there was a box in my bag from my last trip to Vegas.

"I don't care. Use spit if you have to."

Not a chance, but I'm determined to find something that will work.

He's grinding against my thigh, grasping at every part of my skin that he can reach. When his fingers curl around my dick, I know I need to make a decision. "Okay, let me see what I have."

Praying to all the sexual deities out there, I open up my toiletry bag and my shoulders drop. I have a fresh box of condoms and a travel-sized bottle of lube. Looks like we're in business.

Turning back to Pitch, I hold up both prized possessions to show him. "Lookie what I have."

"Thank fuck." He throws the blanket off his body and flips onto his hands and knees, presenting his perfect ass to me. "Hurry up, wouldya."

Where did his boxers go? They're not on the ground, so they must be wadded up at the bottom of my bed. Fuck, he's hot!

With just a few fingertips under the waistband, I push my boxers over my ass and they drop to the ground as I stalk toward my prey. He's so fucking sexy, that pretty pucker just begging for me.

Instead of spreading him open with my fingers, I drop to my knees and kiss his quivering hole. Pitch gasps in shock but pushes back against my mouth, inviting me to dig even deeper.

With my tongue, I trace around his opening before poking my way in, getting a taste of his manly flavor as I squeeze the base of my cock to keep from shooting my load into the side of the mattress.

When I come, I want it to be inside his ass. Which means, I can't delay this much longer.

Without moving my mouth very far away, I shove my finger inside him, working him with just saliva for a few seconds before I pull out and lube up my fingers. Once I'm ready to really get started, I stand up and flip him onto his back.

"Wha–?" He catches his breath without letting go of his perfect cock.

I haven't even gotten a good look at it yet so I gently nudge his hand away and lean down to give it a quick taste. At first, just sucking the tip as if it were a straw and then dragging my tongue all the way down his shaft and up his belly before I stand up in front of him. "I want to watch you while you come."

"Well, I want to come, so get to it already." His hand inches toward his dick, but I raise an eyebrow, silently telling him not to touch it, and he obeys.

"Patience, babe. Let me enjoy this for a few more minutes, because once I start, it's gonna be over way too fast."

As if remembering that I have a dick too, Pitch's eyes drop down to my crotch and he gasps. Now his hand is reaching for me.

I consider swatting it away, but I had some fun, so he should be allowed to too. Instead, I press one knee into the mattress beside his hip and get close enough for him to easily grab my cock and stroke it a few times.

"You're really big." His fingers don't even touch around my girth, and I wonder if he's having second thoughts. But when I look at his face, his pupils are blown and he's practically drooling. "Be generous with the lube."

Before I can say anything else, he rocks back and hooks his arms around the inside of his knees, fully opening himself up for me.

Now this is more like the sex-vixen I was expecting to meet.

9

LARSON

Holy shit, I can't believe this is happening.

In the back of my mind, I'm aware of this being a very bad idea. And my brother's face keeps popping into my head like a devil on my shoulder. But I don't give a shit about any of that right now.

Right now, the only thing that matters to me is how quickly Reed can get that cannon of his into my ass. I haven't had sex in over a year, and all those months of celibacy seem to be culminating into desperation and need like I've never felt in my life.

"Reed, please." I just need him inside me. "I'm ready."

He chuckles and pulls his fingers away from my ass as he repositions himself over my body. "You're so tight. I don't want to hurt you."

"It's gonna hurt no matter what." I pressed my dick into his belly, leaving a sticky drop smeared across his hard abs. "You're fucking huge. Stop teasing me already."

Reed puts another dollop of lube on his palm then covers the condom he's put on before pressing into me. Just when his head breaches my ring of muscle, his soft lips cover mine, distracting me from the pain with gentle kisses and whispers of encouragement.

I'm totally lost in him before the quick burst of pain catches up with me as he bottoms out inside me. "Fuck, Reed."

He nibbles along my jaw then licks my earlobe. "I hope that's your new favorite hobby."

I merely nod as he pulls out and pushes back in, setting a steady rhythm that quickly loosens me up.

Once he's moving, my cock thickens up again and I'm almost instantly back to peak arousal. "That's good." I grab my dick and stroke it in time with his thrusts. "Keep doing it just like that."

"Baby, I want to do it like this forever, but you're too fucking hot. I'm gonna blow soon, especially with the way you're clenching me with that tight ass."

A shudder of ecstasy shoots down my spine, making my whole body quake. "Me too, Reed. I'm close."

His pace picks up, and I can't hold on any longer.

I slide my free hand up his chest and pinch his left nipple as I come in thick ribbons across his belly and mine. "God, Reed."

He presses deep inside me, holding steady, with his dick pulsing against my prostate as he comes. "Fuck, babe. You don't have to call me god, but you're definitely my angel."

Time stands still as we both ride the waves of our orgasms, and when Reed drops onto my chest then quickly rolls us both over so I'm sprawled across him, I know this is just the first of many climaxes we'll share.

Now I just need to be honest with him and tell him who I really am.

It's not like he can be mad at me. My lie was to the band and the audience. Everything between me and Reed was true. Authentic. Granted, my name and occupation aren't what he thinks they are, but I don't think he'll hold that against me. At least, that's what I try to convince myself as my eyes drift shut against his neck and I let myself doze off.

I would have slept until morning if I wasn't awoken by Reed trying to untangle himself from me in the middle of the night. "Where are you going?" I roll onto my back and pull the comforter up. Without his body heat radiating onto me, the brisk desert air suddenly surrounds me.

"Gotta piss. Do you want me to get you a water or anything?"

"I'll come with you." I yawn and realize I need to go too. "Actually, I should probably get back to the bus before the guys start to panic."

Reed's smile drops but then he nods. "Yeah, you're probably right. I don't want them to think I'm neglecting my duty to keep you safe."

I smirk, unable to resist a snarky comeback. "You've definitely not neglected my booty, that's for sure."

He leans down and kisses me, softly at first, but it quickly escalates.

When he pulls away, my lower lip juts out in an inadvertent pout. "Hey, what's wrong?"

"Nothing's wrong, babe." He pulls my lip between his and releases it before giving me a quick peck. "But if I don't go now, I'm gonna have an even bigger mess to clean up."

Oh, right. Now I really have to go too. "Fine, let's go."

It takes me a minute to find my underwear, but once we're both dressed, we head out into the night. The area immediately around the tents is fairly quiet, but we can hear the thud of music and partying off in the distance.

We stop by the porta potties and then Reed walks me to the bus. I want to kiss him goodbye, but I can't do that yet. Not while I'm still Pitch. So I just give him a quick hug and whisper, "Thanks," into his ear before heading up into the bus.

It's empty, so I take a quick shower and then crawl into bed. I dig my phone out of my pocket to send Reed a quick note when I see eight messages from Pitch.

Dude, you fucking rocked it! Baller!

Hey, call me.

WTF, Lars. Just fucking call me.

I'm gonna kick your ass when I see you.

Whatev. If you're heading home, turn your ass around. There's a meet-and-greet on Sunday that you need to be at. It's for all of Glass Bay's artists.

Do you know what that means? We got a fucking contract! Why aren't you responding to me?

The only reason I'll forgive you is if you're getting laid. You better be getting fucking laid right now.

You're prolly asleep so call me when you wake up. But not too early. Just know that I told Slade I'll be at the GB tent at noon.

Holy shit, he got the contract. I want to tell Reed, but he's probably already asleep, so I set my alarm for eight and pass out.

What started out as one of the most terrifying days of my life has ended up being one of the best. Not only for me but for my brother. As much of a fuck-up as Pitch can be, he deserves this contract. He's an amazing artist, and I'm happy I've been able to help him when he needed me most.

For the first time in my life, I fall asleep with a smile on my face.

10

REED

When I fell asleep last night, I was on top of the world. Despite my better judgment, I hooked up with a client, and I thought things were going well. I believed we could actually get something going. Of course, I wasn't thinking about the logistics of him being about to sign a recording contract or that he lives in a different state.

Those were just details.

Today, the details slap me in the face and remind me why I'm not an optimist. Shit is never as easy as it seems. That attitude serves me well in my line of work. I need to always be thinking about the worst-case scenario and how things can go wrong.

And the call I wake up to is my worst-case scenario.

"Dude, what happened? Did he ditch you?" Erin is basically screaming in my ear. "The client is freaking out."

"What?" I jump out of bed and start stepping into clothes. "What happened? Is Pitch okay?" It's only seven in the morning and I dropped him off at two. How much trouble could he have gotten into in five hours?

"You obviously haven't seen the pictures I sent. Check your phone and call me back. We need a story for the client. They're threatening to sue us for breach of contract."

What the fuck? I disconnect the call and open the texts.

There is a stream of photos of Pitch surrounded by women. In one, he's shirtless and kissing a woman while another is on her knees. You can't see his dick out or anything, but it's definitely suggested.

And he isn't wearing his arm brace. Motherfucker! I knew he was using his fingers more than he should if he were really injured. What the hell is going on?

I finish getting dressed and call Erin back as I head toward the bus. "When were these pictures taken?"

She sighs. "They were posted a few hours ago but supposedly from last night. Where is he now?"

"Excellent question. He was in his bus by two, and I was with him the entire time after the show until then. He must have taken off after that." Which makes no sense at all. He was exhausted and tucked right in for the night. Why would he leave after that? Unless the band came back and rounded him up and he had to play the part? I want to give him the benefit of the doubt, but the knot in my gut makes me want to puke. "I'm at his bus now. I'll figure it out."

Hanging up, I take a deep breath and hold my fist over the door to knock. And then I decide against it and just barge in, swinging open the door and letting myself in.

Everyone is asleep. The bus is silent, and Pitch is cuddled up exactly as I left him. What the hell is going on?

I consider waking him up but then remember my place. I'm not his boyfriend. He never made any promises to me. If he went out and got some pussy last night, that's his business. Why should I have expected anything different?

As quietly as possible, I back out of the bus and text Erin. ***He's asleep in the bus. The whole band is passed out. At least for now, he's secure. Isn't the gig over, anyway? Why does the studio care if he partied last night?***

She responds immediately, probably getting a cramp in her thumbs with how fast she must be pecking it out. ***They're signing the contract tomorrow and have to be present and presentable for a meet-and-greet. He's got to behave for another twenty-four hours. After that, escort him off the premises and he'll be someone else's problem.***

They got the contract. Damn. Despite being pissed off and hurt, I'm really happy for him. HIs life is about to change in ways I can't even begin to imagine...and he deserves to enjoy every second of it. Without drama from me. ***Got it.***

All the fight in me fizzles out, and I go back into professional mode of all work and no play. Last night was a fun one-night indulgence, but it shouldn't have happened and it won't happen again. Clearly.

Now that I'm officially back on the clock until after the meet-and-greet tomorrow, I head to the food truck and grab coffee and a burrito. If the guys were partying all night long, they won't be waking up for a while. And truthfully, the later they sleep in, the less I have to deal with Pitch. So if he sleeps for the next twenty-four hours, I'll be happy.

Once I'm parked in front of the bus again, I settle in for a long day. When Pitch wakes up, I'll be friendly and professional. I'm not even gonna mention the photos. If he wants to tell me about his night out, he can. If he doesn't, that's his business. My business is keeping him safe and out of photos in compromising positions.

Obviously, I failed in that aspect last night. Today, he won't be able to shake me as easily. If I have to stay awake and by his side until he's on a plane home, then I'll do it. I've stayed awake much longer than that on jobs that were much more physically demanding.

It'll be simple.

11

LARSON

I wake up and stretch as far as the tiny bunk will allow. My body is sore in all the places that remind me of last night with Reed. A smile blooms across my face as I think about that sexy man inside me, kissing and holding me as if I truly matter to him.

I wonder if he's up yet? Feeling around the bed, I find my phone in my pocket with a dead battery. I guess I forgot to plug it in last night. Oh well. That just means that instead of calling to let him know I'm awake, I can surprise Reed with coffee and breakfast in his tent.

His tent...

If he's still asleep, maybe he'll let me climb in with him and we can pick up where we left off last night.

The other guys are snoring, and it's only nine, so they'll probably be asleep for a few more hours. I heard them come in early this morning, but I didn't bother to look at the time. I was physically, mentally, and emotionally exhausted last night.

But now that I've had some sleep and the worst is behind me, I feel well rested and ready for my day with Reed.

I'll have to tell him about the contract, but I feel guilty celebrating my brother's accomplishment. On the other hand, I can't exactly act like I am not excited or that'll be even more sketch.

Fucking Pitch.

He's the only person in this world that I ever have to lie for, and I hate it. Then again, if it weren't for this particular lie, I wouldn't have met Reed. With a smile back on my face, I grab a clean change of clothes and slip into the bathroom for a quick shower.

The hot water feels nice on my joints, but it runs out quickly, so I don't linger for long. Once I'm dressed again, I step out of the bus to grab food for us at the food trucks.

To my surprise, Reed is leaning against the wall in a shady spot. "Good morning."

"Oh, you're here. How long have you been waiting?"

He shrugs and looks forward, checking out the people passing by, as if he's avoiding eye contact. "I got here a few hours ago. What's on the agenda for today?"

I want to give him a hug and maybe sneak a quick kiss, but the way his arms are tightly crossed over his chest and his lack of eye contact makes me wonder if he has some regrets about last night. Instead of pushing the subject, I take a step back and put some more space between us.

"Well, it sounds like we're getting a contract, so we have a signing tomorrow and a meet-and-greet thing for all the Glass Bay artists. Today is pretty much open."

He nods but doesn't look at me. "I heard about the contract. Congrats. You guys deserve it." He looks at his watch and glances at me. "Are you hungry? I ate earlier, so we can go get whatever you want."

Disappointment fills me, and I wonder if I've done something to piss him off. He seems so distant and aloof, completely different from last night.

It's like he's a different person. *Ironic, isn't it? Clearly karma is punishing me for my lies.*

Suddenly, my appetite is gone. "I'm not really hungry, but coffee would be good."

Reed nods once and pushes off the side of the bus then takes long strides toward the food trucks.

I have to jog a little to keep up with him. "Is everything okay? You seem a little...upset?"

"Nope. I'm good. Just doing my job."

Something's obviously bothering him, but he clearly doesn't want to talk about it. Maybe he's mad that he had to wait for me so long. "I don't know if you tried texting me, but I left my phone off the charger last night, so it's dead."

"Nope, didn't text." His words are short and he seems annoyed at me.

I stop walking and wait for him to stop too and turn toward me. "Did I do something to piss you off? I don't understand why you're mad."

"You didn't do a thing." He shrugs and looks over my shoulder, still not looking me in the eye. "You're a single dude with the world at his fingertips. You're allowed to do anything you want."

I don't even know what that means. I want to ask, but Reed has already turned around and started marching toward the coffee truck. *Okay, I guess he woke up on the wrong side of the bed today. Maybe he just needs some time to work some stuff out.*

Since he obviously doesn't want to be around me right now, I take my coffee back to the bus and tell him I'll text when I plan to leave. I want to say more, maybe make some plans to watch some of the main shows with him, but now doesn't feel like the right time. Hopefully things will cool down later.

When I get back on the bus, Whip is toasting a bagel. "Damn, you were up early."

I almost say that I'm always up early but then I remember that I'm Pitch, and he doesn't get up before noon unless the building's on fire. "Yeah, had to piss then decided to go get some coffee." I take a drink from my cup as if proving my point.

He finishes his bagel and plops down onto the couch. "Can you fucking believe it? A goddamn contract."

I grin at his enthusiasm. I really am proud of these guys. "Yeah, pretty amazing."

"Is everything okay with you, Pitch?" Whip says around a mouthful of bread. "You've been acting a little...different lately. We didn't even see you at all last night."

"Yeah, just..." I look around the bus as if a valid excuse is going to appear from the faux wood paneling. Then I remember the brace on my arm and hold it up. "My arm has been hurting like hell, and the meds they gave me knock me out. I'll be back to normal soon enough."

He laughs and takes another bite. "Well, don't change anything on my account. You were crazy good yesterday. Better than ever. Whatever they're giving you, keep taking it."

Slade appears In the narrow hallway then disappears into the bathroom.

I guess I'm hanging out with the guys today.

"Foo Fighters are up soon. Are you coming with us?" Rocco is leaning down into my cubby with a beer in his hand.

"Yeah." I grab my phone off the charger and realize I missed a call from my brother. "Actually, I need to make a call first. I'll meet you guys there."

"Yeah, good luck with that. Later."

As soon as the guys take off, I call Pitch.

He picks up on the second ring, breathing heavily into the phone. In a whispered voice, he says, "What?"

Asshole. "What do you mean *what*? You called me. I'm just calling you back."

"Oh, fuck. God!" He's grunting, and I can hear motion in the background. "Right, Lars. Hold on. I'm almost done."

"Done with what? What are you doing?"

He groans and speaks between his teeth. "A cute little ginger."

There's a high-pitched voice in the background, and he laughs. "And her mom. Not a ginger but also very cute."

"You are such a fucking pig."

Pitch just laughs. "Yeah, so? How's it going?"

"Call me when you're done." I hit the disconnect button and open up Instagram. I try not to spend too much time on social media, but my curiosity is getting the better of me, and I can't avoid messages about the show any longer. As cringy as it sounds, I kinda want to know what people think of my performance.

Everything about the show is positive. The comments are all kind and everyone loved Pitch. Most are saying it was his best performance yet.

If he were anyone else, I would worry that he might feel threatened by the fact that people are saying my show was better than any of his. But my brother doesn't think that way. He's narcissistic enough to never let it occur to him that somebody could be better than him.

He'll consider last night's win his and own it like everything else in his world.

I scroll through the messages, and my stomach drops when I recognize a familiar name.

Mandy_RockGRL is his ex. The crazy ex he has a restraining order against. This woman thought he was going to marry her someday, but Pitch never wanted her for more than a booty call.

When they broke up for good, she didn't take it well.

We didn't think her threats were legit until she set his car on fire. Fortunately, he wasn't in it and no one was hurt, but she's not supposed to be within fifty feet of him. But according to the photo she posted from the airport last night, she was boarding a plane to Reno at 9PM. Which means, she might be here now.

I call my brother again, hoping he's finished with his friends from earlier.

"Hey, Lars. I was just about to call you back."

"Whatever. Mandy is here. At the show. At least, that's what she posted last night."

"Fuck!" I hear rustling in the background and female voices. "Dude, you need to stay the hell away from her. If you see her at all, get security to arrest her."

There is some music playing in the background, and it sounds suspiciously like the music I can hear coming through the walls of the bus. "Where are you?"

"The less you know the better." He laughs at what he apparently thinks is a joke. "Okay, you caught me. I'm here, but I'm incognito. Don't worry. No one will see me."

"Dude, what the fuck? I don't wanna be the asshole who lied to all these fans yesterday. You cannot be seen here. Or...just be Pitch again. I'll leave now, and you can come out as yourself. I'll leave the arm brace here. Just slip it on and tell people you lost your voice last night."

"Dude, can you hear me? I sound like shit. I can't risk not getting the contract because the studio thinks I have vocal issues."

"Then why the fuck are you risking not getting the contract, Pitch? You need to be smarter than this. Couldn't you just stay away for one more day?"

"Dude, relax. Seriously, no one will recognize me. I just want to hear some of our competition."

I should have expected him to pull some shit like this. He can never sit out a good time. He has to be where the action is, even if it could destroy his whole career. And in this case, he'd be taking me down with him.

"Whatever. If shit goes down, I'm leaving, and I'm never talking to you again."

He laughs, clearly not buying my bluff. "Yeah, whatever. Thanks again, Lars. You were really great yesterday."

I hang up the phone and don't even bother looking at the rest of the comments about Pitch Monroe. Whatever shit he's gotten himself into, there's nothing I can do but wait it out.

And with Reed in a mood, it looks like I'll be waiting it out by myself.

I go to the couch and grab the remote. Maybe there's a House Hunters International marathon playing today.

At least I can fantasize about being anywhere but here.

12

REED

I've been on some boring jobs in my time, but sitting outside the bus is torture.

My dick wants me to go inside and hang out with Pitch now that he's alone. But my mind is forcing me to keep my feet planted right where they are. Any unnecessary interaction between us is just going to hurt more when we go our separate ways tomorrow.

The sun is setting, and a glare from the neighbor's bus is shining right at me, so I cross the walkway and find a spot near a water station. I still have a clear view of the front and side of the bus, so Pitch won't sneak past me. But from here, I don't have to deal with the sun blinding me for the next fifteen minutes.

There are a lot more people coming and going today, more so than the previous few days. I know that's because the show is winding down, but it gets my nerves on heightened alert.

A woman walks past me in an oversized hoodie and a black hat with sunglasses on, even though the walkway is well shaded. She seems jumpy as she looks all around, and then she stops in front of Pitch's bus.

Standing at the door, she looks like she's deciding whether or not to knock. If this is one of his booty calls, I certainly don't want to scare her away. It's his life. If he wants a piece of her, he's allowed to get some.

I step back into the shadow of a nearby rig and take a drink of my Gatorade as I watch from around the corner.

The woman looks in both directions and then squares her shoulders as if she's made a decision. But instead of knocking on the door, she pulls open one of the storage panels on the side of the bus until she finds the propane tanks.

My spidey senses are on alert, but if she's just some obnoxious fan, wanting to leave a teddy bear for one of the guys, I don't want to overreact. I watch her open her purse and dig around for something, and then she suddenly shoves something inside and quickly stands up and walks in the same direction she came from.

"Hey there." I call out to her. "Hold on a second."

She turns to me and then starts to run.

I have a decision to make. I can either chase after her and ask what she's doing, or I can go and see for myself. With Pitch alone inside that bus, that seems like the most reliable choice.

I take off toward the bus and open the panel. The door pops right open, and I can see a glass bottle with gold liquid in the back of it. There is a long towel taped around the top and it's slowly smoldering toward the bottle like a fuse.

I dump my Gatorade on the burning end to put it out then run inside and grab Pitch.

He's sprawled on the couch, surprised to see me. "Hey, Ree—"

I don't let him finish his sentence before he's in my arms and over my shoulder. "There's a bomb. We've got to get out of here." I carry him out of the bus, and he just curls into me, not even questioning me at all.

Once we're a safe distance away from the bus, I put him down and call the on-site fire department for backup.

Pitch listens quietly as I explain the situation to the fire marshal, then the head of security, and finally, Erin. While I'm giving her an update of what just happened, Pitch drops to the ground at the realization of just how close he was to death.

I don't have anything warm for him to wear, but he looks like he's going into shock. Without any other option, I sit down behind him and wrap my arms around his body. "You're okay, Pitch. Everything's good now. You're safe."

He's still silent, breathing soft and steady.

I'm not sure he's said a single word since I pulled him out of that bus, and it's starting to scare me. "Pitch, baby. Please talk to me. Tell me you're okay."

"I'm not." He's hardly audible, but I can hear the dejection in his tone.

"What?" I sit back and look him over to make sure there's not some injury I missed or maybe even caused. Physically, he looks fine, but mentally, he's about to break.

Suddenly, the bus is surrounded by firetrucks and ambulance vans, so I get him to his feet and we walk toward the closest ambulance.

As soon as a paramedic sees us, I quickly explain what happened and get Pitch settled on the tailgate of their van. As they begin their evaluation, I bend down so I can look him in the eyes. "I'll be right back."

Pitch looks at me and his mouth opens like he wants to say something, but he doesn't. He just drops his gaze and nods.

I turn to the paramedic and lean close to his ear. "Don't let him out of your sight. I'll be back in two minutes." Then I jog over to the fire marshal and show them what I found.

It doesn't take them long to confirm that the propane tank was disconnected from the gas line to the bus and fumes were escaping into the storage compartment. The bottle I saw was in fact a homemade bomb. It's amateurish, something any kid could make from watching a YouTube video, but with the open gas tank, the entire bus would've exploded if it hadn't been extinguished.

They need some time to do a full inspection of the bus to make sure there aren't any other explosives, so I head back to check on Pitch. He's curled up in a ball but speaking to the paramedic, so I know he's going to be alright.

I lift my hand toward him, giving him the opportunity to stop me, but he doesn't.

He just looks at me and then nods as I step closer. Within seconds, my arms are wrapped around him, and he's clinging to me, sobbing against my chest. "I could have died. But you saved me."

I rest my cheek against his temple. "You're safe now, baby. No one's going to hurt you."

"But you didn't have to." He sniffs and his voice gets stronger. "You were so mad at me. I don't even know why."

"I don't know why either." I close my eyes and kiss the side of his head. "Don't worry about that. I'm not mad at you."

He pulls back and looks up at me. "Really? Are you sure?"

I grin and rest my forehead against his before finally releasing him and stepping away. "I promise. I just had a rough morning. Some work shit. I'm sorry I took it out on you."

All the tension in his shoulders releases on an exhale. "Thank God. I thought things went really well last night, and I woke up in such a good mood. And then..."

I want to keep the mood light, but I can't stop myself from getting back to what I really want to know. "Why did you leave?"

"What are you talking about? For coffee? My phone was dead. I told you that."

I cross my arms over my chest, reflexively building a wall between us. "Last night. After you went to bed, why did you go back out without telling me?"

He shakes his head. "I didn't. I went to sleep and didn't get up until—"

"Don't." I raise my hand between us, stopping him mid-lie. "Don't lie to me, Pitch. I saw the pictures of you. Look, you're an adult and you're allowed to do whatever you want. I'm not mad about that. But you should have told me. Something like this could've happened last night."

I can see the wheels turning in his head, and his expression changes completely. "Did you see pictures of me partying last night?"

"Yeah." I dare him to deny it now that *he knows* that *I know*.

He sighs heavily and then throws his head back. "Fucking Pitch."

Uh, excuse me? "What?"

"My brother. Pitch Monroe." He takes a deep breath then looks me in the eyes. "I'm Larson. His twin. He begged me to pretend to be him this weekend because he fucked up his throat and couldn't perform. He promised he'd keep a low profile so I could get through these few days without incident, but he can't keep it in his fucking pants and has apparently been screwing his way through the state."

"You're not Pitch?" Nothing makes sense, but then everything sorta does. Other than how he looks and how he sings, he's nothing like the Pitch Monroe I've seen in the spotlight. "Why didn't you tell me sooner?"

"I almost did...so many times. But I wanted you to have plausible deniability in case I got caught. I didn't want to take you down with me, so I figured I'd wait until this weekend was over and...if you were still talking to me, I would come clean. I'm sorry."

13

LARSON

By the time we're allowed back on the bus, it's late and I'm spent.

Reed walks me inside to grab my bag, and I realize my phone's been there the whole time. It rings the second I pull it off the charger. It's Pitch.

Now it's my turn to be pissed off by the interruption. "What?"

"Dude, are you okay? I heard there was an explosion or some shit by your bus. What happened?"

I roll my eyes and put it on speaker for Reed to hear. "Your psycho ex tried to blow up the fucking bus. I was the only one on it but Reed extinguished the molotov cocktail and got me out. That's what fucking happened, Pitch."

"Fuck, Lars. Are you really okay? And who the hell is Reed?"

I roll my eyes. "He's your babysitter. The studio hired him to keep you alive. And good thing they did because, surprise, surprise, he had to do exactly that."

"I'm almost at the bus. Just wait for me." I can hear the music getting louder, like he's out of whatever shelter he was in.

"I'm not there anymore." I nod toward the door and follow Reed outside. "I'm heading to Reed's tent. You can meet me there. It's..."

"303." Reed mouths his tent number as he takes my bag and places his arm behind my back. It's dark now, so neither of us are worried about who sees Pitch Monroe in the arms of another man.

"Tent 303. I'll be there for the rest of the night." When Reed raises an eyebrow at me, I wink, inviting myself to stay for a sleepover. His reciprocating grin is all the invitation I need.

We get to his tent at the same time Pitch does.

"Dude, Lars." He pulls me to his chest and wraps me in a bear hug. He's a lot more muscular than I am, so I'm basically a rag doll in his arms. "I'm so glad you're okay."

"I can't breathe, Pitch."

He laughs and releases his grip on me. "Sorry. I was just worried when I heard about the explosion."

Reed steps forward and holds out his hand. "Reed Marshall. I take it you're the real Pitch Monroe?"

He grins coyly. "Yeah, that's me. Sorry for the Freaky Friday shit. I just needed some help from my bro."

I pull the brace off my arm and hold it out to him. "This is yours. Put it on. You're officially Pitch again. I'm off-duty."

He looks at me and then down at the brace. "Yeah, you're right. I'll tell them the smoke irritated my throat and that's why I can't talk."

Reed laughs. "There wasn't actually a fire, man. A bomb was placed in the bus, but it didn't go off. No smoke."

Pitch just shrugs. "Yeah, whatever. I'll think of something. Anyway, I'll let you guys get back to..." He looks around the tent and grins. "Whatever it is you're about to get up to. I've got fans to please."

As soon as we're alone, Reed turns me around in his arms. "So, Larson Monroe, it's nice to meet you."

I smile and rest my head on his chest. "I'm sorry for not telling you sooner. I hope you understand."

"I do." He leans down and kisses me, brushing his lips against mine. "And that's in the past."

Now I laugh out loud. "The past, as in twenty minutes ago?"

Reed shrugs. "As in before you almost died. Now that you're back and I know you weren't fucking around with some hot roadies last night, I'm in a forgiving mood."

"Oh yeah?" I press my pelvis against his so our cocks are aligned. "Wanna know what kind of mood I'm in?"

Reed laughs and drops his hands to my ass, cupping each cheek in his strong hands. "I think I can guess."

"Well, can you guess naked? Because that's how I want you. Now." I slip my hand under his shirt and walk my fingertips over the ridges and valleys of his abs.

He does the same, slipping his hand under my shirt. "Does this mean I get to see you without a shirt?"

"Oh, yeah." I rip my shirt over my head and then quickly strip out of my pants. "No more secrets."

Reed stands over me, getting his first look at my unmarked skin. "You're absolutely beautiful."

"Yeah?" I run my hand over my chest and down my belly. "Not too boring for you?"

He slowly takes off his clothes, making sure my eyes track every movement. He's hot as fuck as his shirt comes off and those tight muscles are revealed. And then his pants drop, and he's totally naked. Like a wolf stalking his prey, he plants one knee on the mattress and then the other, sliding over my body like he's claiming it.

God, I want him to claim me. Want me. Keep me.

"No more lies, Larson." His tone is low and calm, leaving no room for negotiation on this matter.

I clear my throat and nod. "No more lies."

He rubs his nose across mine and kisses me, just a tease before he pulls back and looks at me with lustful eyes. Then he kisses my chin, slowly working his way across my neck, over my chest, and down to where I really want him.

My cock is hard and already leaking when he finally drags his tongue over the tip.

"Delicious."

I groan and thrust up, silently begging him to take it all.

His tongue draws a line down my shaft and then back up before he presses his closed lips against my tip and pushes down, making me squeeze through the tight, wet opening.

"Oh fuck. Reed, it's too good."

He hums his agreement as he slowly licks all around my dick.

I fist the comforter, using it to hold myself in place so I don't attach myself to him. Patience has never been one of my virtues. "Now, Reed. I'm going to come now."

He picks up his pace, sliding up and down my shaft even faster. He wraps his fingers in a ring around the base of my dick then sliding up, meeting his lips with every thrust. His wet fingers then cup my balls, and I lose it.

"Yes, Reed." My whole body arches up, and he swallows the head of my dick, taking my offering straight down his throat.

Instead of pulling off immediately, he continues to suck me as I shrink in his mouth. When he's only got the head of my cock between his lips, sucking me like a lollipop, I start to get hard all over again.

He grins around my dick before finally releasing me and sliding back up my body until our mouths are connected, and I can taste myself on him. His dick is hard as steel as it presses against my flesh.

"Your turn?"

He closes his eyes and moans as he repositions his dick so it's closer to my opening. "My turn. Your turn. Is there a difference?"

I roll my hips, loving the way his velvety skin feels as it presses against my hole. "No difference. Just hurry up and take your turn so I can have another."

"Okay, okay. I guess Larson is the bossy twin..."

I shrug and reach for one of his nipples, squeezing it between my fingertips. "Only when you take your sweet time getting inside me."

"We've got all night, baby. No need to rush."

14

REED

Last night was another amazing night with Pit... Larson. It's going to take me some time to get used to that, but now that I know the truth, it seems so obvious. How could anyone mistake either of them for the other?

They are completely different men. And having met them together just one time, I already know I could instantly tell them apart.

My Larson is sweet and kind and generous.

The real Pitch is arrogant and self-centered—not at all like his brother.

Speaking of his brother, my fingers comb through his soft hair, playing with it as he sleeps. Larson is a heavy sleeper. The only time he seemed to wake up at all was when I shifted out from under him because I had a cramp in my calf.

But since he settled beside me, he's been down for the count.

It's almost ten on Sunday, so we have all day, but I'm kinda anxious to get out of here. Not to leave him, but just to be with him in a different place.

A new start, if you will.

"If you press a little harder, that will be an amazing scalp massage." His sleepy voice makes me smile as I lean forward and kiss his forehead. "Good morning."

"It is a good morning, isn't it?" He lifts his head and puckers up for a kiss on the lips.

I happily oblige, starting off chaste and then quickly deepening it because I just can't get enough of him.

Larson rolls to the side and presses his morning wood against my thigh. "I'm happy to see you."

I grin and reach for his dick, teasing it with a few soft strokes. "I can feel how happy you are." I grab my cock with the same hand and stroke us together.

“I’m happy to see you too.” Soft and lazy strokes, just enough to feel good without coming yet.

We lie like that for a while before we finally give in and I stroke with more purpose. It doesn’t take long for us to come against each other, both of us releasing at the same time amid gentle touches and rough kisses.

I bask in the moment, not caring at all about the puddle we’re now lying in. “I think this is the best wake-up call I’ve ever had.”

He chuckles against me and burrows into my chest. “This is definitely my best wake-up call.”

Larson’s stomach grumbles, and I realize neither of us ate last night. “You must be starving.”

Larson holds his breath as if thinking about it, and then cocks his head to the side. “Yeah, I think I am.”

I chuckle and give him a quick peck before rolling to the side and hopping out of bed. “We can leave these sticky sheets for someone else to deal with. “How about we get something to eat and then get out of here.”

He opens his mouth to speak but then closes it and just nods.

"Is that okay?"

"Yeah, that's good. I need food, and one last breakfast burrito sounds perfect."

He doesn't say much while we get dressed and head toward the food trucks. Something has changed with Larson in just a few minutes, but he walks with his arm curled around mine and his sleeves pushed up, probably so nobody mistakes him for his brother.

We grab food and coffee then sit down at the same table we were at for our last meal together.

That's when he finally opens up. "So, what happens now? Like, when we leave here today."

Right...*the conversation*. "Well, I have the week off. I always get the week off after a job that lasts more than 36 hours, so I'm not in a hurry to get home."

His eyes brighten and the smile I've become addicted to appears on his perfect face. "I'm off work too. This weekend was a surprise, and I didn't know what else I might need to do after the event, so I took the whole week off. Besides, I have a ton of vacation time saved up, so it was a good excuse to use some."

"Nice." I thought about our options as I took a bite of my burrito. Then inspiration struck. "Well, there's a spa resort in Reno that's pretty nice. They have Roman baths and comfortable beds. Maybe we can spend a few days there, if you'd like."

"Yes." He responds without hesitating but then catches himself and tries to pull back. "I mean, if you want to. I know this has been a quick...whatever this is. And it's almost like you're just meeting me as Larson for the first time..."

I hold up my hand to stop him. "I know the real Larson. I don't know the real Pitch, but other than the moments you were on stage or with the rest of the band, you were *you*. And *you* are exactly who I want to spend some time with."

His grin is infectious, and I want to pull him onto my lap and kiss him till we're both breathless. But now isn't the time or the place.

Larson finally takes a bite, and his eyes roll back in appreciation. "How do these get better every time?"

I mumble in agreement around my own big bite. "The cheese they put in these is delicious."

After a few minutes of focused eating time, he takes a breath and looks at me. "So, you live in Vegas right?" I can see the fear of our reality setting into Larson's face.

I hate that he's worried about anything. "Yes, and you live in L.A. That's a pretty short drive. Just a few hours."

He nods. "Yeah, I guess."

"Ya know, we get on-site assignments in L.A. all the time. If you ever feel like you're not seeing me often enough, I could probably take one of those and be enough that you'll be sick of me before you know it." I wink before taking a drink of my coffee.

He cocks his head and smirks. "I can't imagine ever getting tired of you, but I can also work at home most of the time. My office has a lot of remote workers in other states, so I'm flexible too."

"Flexible, huh? Maybe we need to get a little more creative so I can see some of these acrobatics?"

Larson laughs out loud, probably imagining what that might look like. In my mind, he's the only one who comes out looking good in that scenario. "I don't think acrobatics is the right word, but...I might have a few more moves you haven't seen yet."

I glance at my watch dramatically and then put my burrito down and begin to wrap it up. "Well let's get on the road, baby. We're burning daylight here."

15

LARSON

After an amazing week of staying in bed, having room service delivered, and falling head over heels for Reed, I don't ever wanna go home. The bubble we've been living in is bliss, and I know that once we both go our separate ways, everything will change.

Not that we aren't both committed to making a long-distance relationship work. I think we are. But I'm already addicted to curling up with him at night and waking up to his kisses in the morning. How can I go back to my lonely apartment after this?

"Why the frown?" Reed has his laptop open but he's looking right at me.

I huff out a breath. "I don't want to go home."

He closes his laptop and puts it on the nightstand, then he pulls me against his chest and lowers us to the mattress. "I don't want to either, but it's only for a few days. I'm going to be at your place on Saturday morning, and I should be able to stay for the whole weekend."

"I know." I don't like to pout, but I find myself doing it more than a grown man should ever be allowed to. "But I like this." My arms tighten around his chest as I squeeze him. "You're like my new favorite pillow."

He moans as if that's a painful thing to hear. "I know, baby. I'm going to miss you too. But I'm gonna call you every chance I get, and talk to you while you fall asleep, and be your wake-up call every morning..."

"Can't you just live with me?" My eyes go wide the second I realize what just came out of my mouth. "I mean... Well, can't you?"

Reed chuckles beneath me, rubbing shapes on my back.

I focus on his fingertips and realize it's not just any shape. It's a heart.

"I want to, baby. And don't be surprised if I arrive at your house on Saturday morning with a U-Haul truck because I'm falling for you in a way I never have for anyone else."

I lift my head to look him in the eyes. "Me too. I've never been in love before, but I think this is what it feels like."

Reed leans forward and presses his lips to mine as he nods against me. "That's definitely what it feels like for me."

We sit quietly in each other's arms for a long time before Reed finally lifts me up so I'm sitting on his lap and we're both upright. "How about we go for a hike? There are some nice trails around here, and we could probably use some fresh air after being stuck to this bed for a week."

I chuckle and lift my arm to stretch it out. "Yeah, I think my muscles are beginning to atrophy. Well, most of them, at least." I waggle my eyebrows at him. "There are a couple that have been well exercised this week."

"It's settled then." He smacks my ass and then bounces me onto the mattress beside him before standing up and walking toward the bathroom. "Let's get cleaned up and we can make the most of the day before I have to take you to the airport."

"Ugh, don't remind me about that." I follow him to the bathroom, and we shower together. Of course, we have to dirty ourselves up even more before getting clean, but we eventually make it out of the resort.

It's a beautiful day with just enough sun in the sky that we're comfortable in T-shirts and jeans. Neither of us have actual hiking shoes, so we stick to a beginner trail and just casually meander through the foothills.

After a few hours of exploring, we stop at a cute little restaurant for lunch. When we're done eating, I lean back in my seat and sigh. "It's almost time, isn't it?"

Reed glances at his watch and nods. "This isn't goodbye, babe. I'm not letting you get away that easily." He reaches across the table and opens his hand.

I place mine in his and give it a squeeze.

His eyes are locked with mine and I couldn't look away if I wanted to. "This is new for both of us, but that doesn't mean it isn't real. Some people might say we're being impulsive, and that's okay. I know what I want, and I want you. I love you."

"I love you too, Reed. And I want this to work. I'll do anything to make this work. Whatever it takes."

We're making big statements and big promises, but they don't feel wrong. It feels exactly right.

Before I'm ready, we have to head to the airport.

I returned my rental car on our way into Reno, so Reed drives me to the airport in his SUV. He holds my hand the entire drive, drawing figure-eights with his thumb over my skin.

As unexpected as this whole week has been, I know we'll figure out a way to make things work between us.

I've had boyfriends in the past, but never like this. No one like Reed.

And I meant what I said about doing anything it takes to make a relationship work.

He parks by my terminal and walks with his arm clutched behind my back as we head in. He doesn't release his tight hold on me until we're at the security line.

I turn to face him with a sad smile. "I'll call you when I land."

He gives me a serious look and furrows his eyebrows. "You'll text when you board so I know when you're in the air. And then, yes, call me when you land."

"Oh, okay." I grin, kinda turned on by the fact that he wants to make sure I'm safe.

I've always been the independent one in my family. Because Pitch was such a wild child, he got all the attention while I was "the easy one" as my mom likes to say.

Reed holds me against his chest for a long time before finally letting go and taking a step back. "I love you, Larson, and I'll see you soon."

I can feel tears welling but I don't let them fall as I suck in a deep breath through my nose. "I love you too, Reed. I'll talk to you soon."

16

REED

"What the hell's wrong with you?" Baker, my best friend and the one I'm usually assigned to work with, nudges my shoulder while we wait in line at our favorite sandwich shop.

"Just waiting for Saturday."

He rolls his eyes and smirks. "Damn, you've got it bad. I've never seen you this whipped before. What's so special about this guy, anyway?"

I stare into the distance and smile, thinking about all the reasons Larson is so special. "He's sweet and kind and sexy as fuck." I look at my friend and grin. "He knows exactly what I need...when I need it."

Baker laughs. "He's a good lay? That's what this is about?"

"No, he's so much more than that. I mean, yeah, he is. But I really love him. It's crazy. I didn't think it was possible for me."

Baker blows out a low whistle. "Well, goddamn. I never thought I'd see the day either." He pats my back a few times. "I'm happy for you, man. You deserve this."

I shrug and shake my head. "I don't think I deserve him, but I definitely plan on keeping him."

Baker laughs. "Well, that must've been one crazy week."

"You have no idea." So many of our early moments flash in my mind, making me smile even broader.

Baker and I are assigned to a tech conference, mostly keeping press away from CEOs after their keynote talks. That makes for an easy week for us. That's lucky for me and my charges because I have no brain space available for anything except Larson.

He fills every bit of my mind...all day and all night.

And as the week drags by, I'm more and more anxious to see Larson. By Friday afternoon, I'm practically buzzing to get the hell out of town.

I pull out my phone and send him a text. ***Hey, baby. I'm tempted to change my flight and come in tonight.***

Yes!!! he responds immediately. ***I'm not gonna be able to sleep anyway, so you might as well be here to help me get through the night.***

Rebooking now.

It costs a small fortune, but I'm able to get an 8pm flight to LAX. When I arrive, Larson is waiting for me at baggage claim. As soon as I see him, my arms open up for him.

He lunges against my chest and holds me like he hasn't seen me in years instead of days. "I missed you."

I hold him just as tightly, breathing in his coconut shampoo as he melts against me. "I missed you too, baby."

"Do you need to wait for luggage?"

I lift the duffle up to show him. "Nope, I packed light."

He frowns and his lower lip sticks out slightly. "Oh, okay."

Whoa, what just happened. "Is something wrong?"

He lowers his gaze and pulls back. "No, it's fine."

I tug him closer and lift his chin with my finger so he's forced to look me in the eyes. "No more lies, remember?"

Larson sighs and then bites his lip, tucking it back inside his glorious mouth. "I was kinda hoping you'd pack heavily...and stay for a while." He shoots me a half-grin. "Or forever."

"Fuck, baby." How can I ever resist him? "I'm working on it."

"You are?" His eyes light up and he's back to his usual self. "Good. Then let's go work on it at home."

In addition to lots of naked time, Larson shows me around the city he loves. We go to the beach for a few hours after brunch and then head up to the top of Mulholland Drive to watch the sun set. By the time

Sunday afternoon rolls around, I know this is where I need to be for the foreseeable future.

I pull out my phone and send a text to Erin. ***I need to relocate to LA. Are there any assignments coming up that I can get in on?***

Despite it being a weekend, she texts back within a few minutes. ***Cameron has been asking to move back for a few months. Let me see when he can be ready to leave and you guys can swap.***

Thanks, E. I'm gonna stay here a few more days. Let me know when you need me back there.

Will do.

Larson is watching me with hopeful eyes. "Is everything okay?"

I grin and open my arms to him.

He's returning from the kitchen with a few beers, but he drops them onto the coffee table and hops onto my lap. "That smile has to mean good news, right?"

I chuckle and shake my head. "Yes, baby. Good news. I don't have to be at work for a few days, so I can stay."

His arms close around my neck, and Larson peppers kisses across my face. "Thank you, Reed." He shifts his weight so he's now straddling me. "I've been hoping you'd say that all weekend."

I slide my hands down to his ass and cup his cheeks, pressing him closer so his cock is aligned with mine. "Oh yeah? And what are we gonna do with all this extra time?"

He tilts his hips, rubbing against my length with his. "I have a few ideas. I might even break out some of those acrobatics you've been asking about."

"Well, hell. Keep talking like that and I'll never leave."

His pupils get big and he presses his lips to mine, whispering against them. "That's my plan."

EPILOGUE
LARSON

Six months later

My company has officially gone remote in an effort to save costs on empty buildings that nobody ever goes into, so I can go anywhere in the world. But Reed insists on staying in L.A. I love it here, and he loves me...and the weather, so here we are.

The only issue is that my apartment is getting cramped, so we've been doing a lot of house hunting over the past couple months.

An alert from Zillow pings my phone as we're eating breakfast, and I immediately check it out. "Three bedrooms, three bathrooms, a dog kennel in the backyard, and a gourmet kitchen."

Reed looks up from his pancakes. "How does it look?"

I flip through some of the pictures and my jaw drops. "Amazing, actually. Really nice." I turn the phone so he can see the pictures.

"Yeah, that looks pretty good. In our budget?"

I grin. "Surprisingly, it is."

He places his hand on my shoulder and gives me a squeeze. "Well, let's go check it out."

I send a text to our realtor to see if he can meet us out there. Nice houses don't last long in this market, so every minute counts.

As if all our good karma is combining together to make this work for us, our agent is just finishing a showing around the block from the house we want to look at, so we head over.

Fifteen minutes later, we're there and walking through the best house we've seen in months. The house is perfect. There are some things we'll need to change, but the bones are good, and we both fall in love instantly.

I turn to Reed as we stand in the backyard, overlooking the vegetable garden. "What do you think?"

He turns to me with a smirk. "You know what I think. And I know what you think."

I grin widely. "Are we writing an offer?"

He nods and pulls me into his arms. "Hell yeah, we're writing an offer. This is going to be our home."

We bid $15,000 over the asking price, and our offer is accepted. Honestly, I thought we might get into a bidding war, but some bad wallpaper choices seem to have scared off potential buyers.

For me, I saw those walls as opportunities. Opportunities to create the perfect home for Reed and I.

"You excited?" Reed and I are eating pizza on the balcony, watching the sunset.

"About the house?" I curl my legs underneath myself and lean closer to him. "Very. I already have so many ideas of how I want to decorate and what colors to paint each room.

"Well, I'm happy to see you so happy." He takes a deep breath then slides off the chair and lands on one knee in front of me. "And I'm hoping that you'll make me just as happy by agreeing to become my husband."

My jaw drops, and I don't know what to say. I mean, of course the answer is yes, but I'm in shock.

Complete and utter shock.

Reed raises an eyebrow and grins. "Playing hard to get, huh?" He reaches into his pocket and pulls out a little velvet pouch. Then he reaches for my hand and pulls a ring from the pouch. "Does this help sweeten the pot?"

"Yes!" I finally find my voice and throw myself at him.

Reed almost falls backward from my weight, but my man is strong and steady, easily holding me upright when I need him. "Yes?"

"Of course!" I kiss him hard until we're both gasping for breath. "A thousand times yes!"

Reed stands up and carries me with him.

When we're both on our feet, he slips the ring on my finger and then pulls it to his lips for a soft kiss. "I love you, Larson Monroe. And I can't wait to build a home and a life with you."

"I love you too, Reed." I look at the ring and my future husband and feel tears stream down my cheeks. I don't deserve this much happiness and love in my life, but I'm grateful to have it. "Now take me to bed!"

ALSO BY ARIA GRACE

Contemporary M/M Box Sets

- **More Than Friends Full Series**
- **Mile High Romance Books 1-5**
- **Men of the Vault Series**

Contemporary M/M Mpreg

- **Omega House Books 1-5**
- **Omega For Hire Books 1-5**
- **Glass Bay Apartments**

Shifter M/M Mpreg

- **River's Edge Shifters**

And be sure to read all the Road to Rocktober 2022 books

- **Road to Rocktober 2022**

The Road to Rocktoberfest
2022
BLADE
LIGHT
NOISE
HIS TUNE
Three KIND
REUNION
Bleeding DAWN
RHYTHMS
Muted CHORDS
In TUNE
DISASTER
ON ME